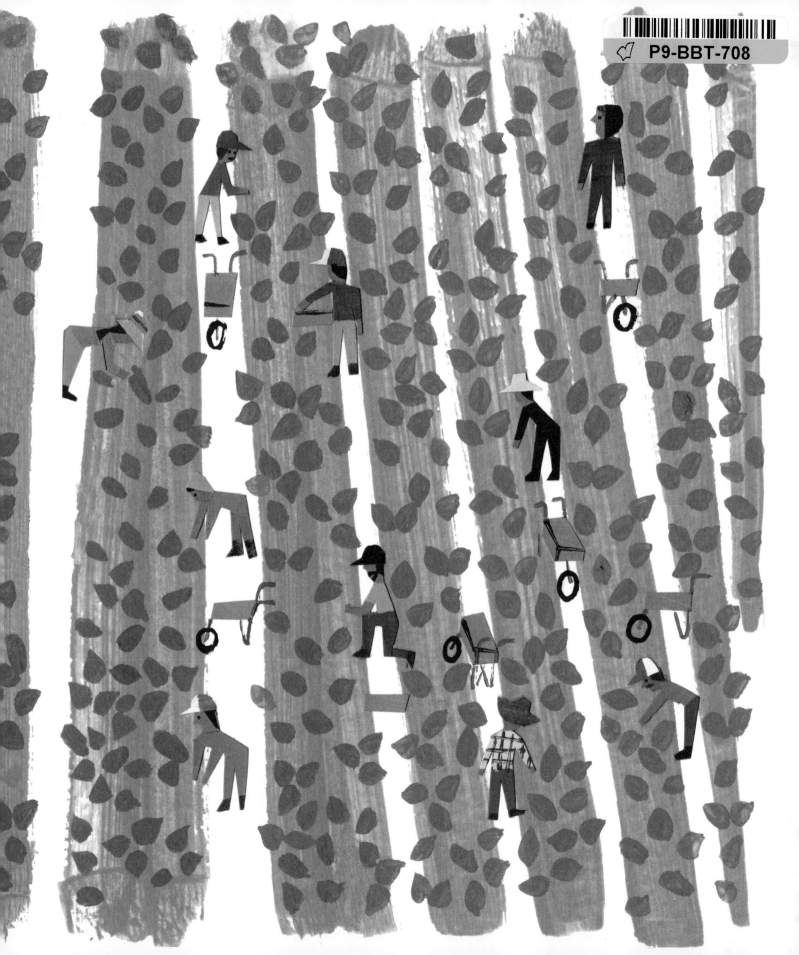

For my grandparents Jesús and Natividad de la Peña
and everyone else who has journeyed to
America with a dream—M. de la P.

For Claudette—C.R.

G. P. PUTNAM'S SONS
an imprint of Penguin Random House LLC
375 Hudson Street, New York, NY 10014

Text copyright © 2018 by Matt de la Peña.
Illustrations copyright © 2018 by Christian Robinson.
Penguin supports copyright. Copyright fuels creativity, encourages diverse voices, promotes free speech, and creates a vibrant culture. Thank you for buying an authorized edition of this book and for complying with copyright laws by not reproducing, scanning, or distributing any part of it in any form without permission. You are supporting writers and allowing Penguin to continue to publish books for every reader.
G. P. Putnam's Sons is a registered trademark of Penguin Random House LLC.
Library of Congress Cataloging-in-Publication Data
Names: de la Peña, Matt, author. | Robinson, Christian, illustrator.
Title: Carmela full of wishes / Matt de la Peña ; Christian Robinson.
Description: New York, NY : G. P. Putnam's Sons, [2018]
Summary: Carmela, finally old enough to run errands with her brother, tries to think of the perfect wish, while his wish seems to be that she stayed home.
Identifiers: LCCN 2017054780 | ISBN 9780399549045 (hardcover) | ISBN 9780399549076 (ebook) | ISBN 9780399549052 (ebook)
Subjects: | CYAC: Wishes—Fiction. | Brothers and sisters—Fiction. | Birthdays—Fiction. | Hispanic Americans—Fiction.
Classification: LCC PZ7.P3725 Car 2018 | DDC [E]—dc23
LC record available at https://lccn.loc.gov/2017054780
Manufactured in China by RR Donnelley Asia Printing Solutions Ltd.
ISBN 9780399549045
1 2 3 4 5 6 7 8 9 10
Design by Eileen Savage. Text set in Paradigm.
The art for this book was created with acrylic paint, collage,
and a bit of digital manipulation.

CARMELA
FULL OF WISHES

Newbery Medal–winning author   Caldecott Honor–winning illustrator
MATT DE LA PEÑA   **CHRISTIAN ROBINSON**

G. P. PUTNAM'S SONS

Carmela scootered along the uneven dirt path,
watching men stoop to work with their hands,
her birthday bracelets jingling and jangling.
The thick greenhouse air smelled of marigolds
and overturned earth
and fresh manure.

Carmela knew exactly what manure was,
but she didn't want to think about that.
Not today.

Today she awoke to candles in her pancakes, and her mom sang, "Happy birthday to you!" and told her, "Go on, mija, make a wish!" But Carmela's wish had already come true. She was finally old enough to go with her big brother.

Carmela followed as he cut back onto the street at Freedom Boulevard,
past the crowded bus stop and fenced-off repair shop,
past the old folks' home where two hunched old women waved smiles,
past the huge home improvement store where her dad used to
stand around weekend mornings, waiting for work.

Carmela tried to make small talk with her brother as their
metal cart rattled, but her brother didn't make small talk back.
He didn't want her tagging along.
Too bad! she told him with her glare.

Just outside the Laundromat, she picked a lone dandelion
growing among the concrete weeds.
She pulled a breath and leaned toward the fuzzy white bulb,
but just before she could blow, her brother butted in.

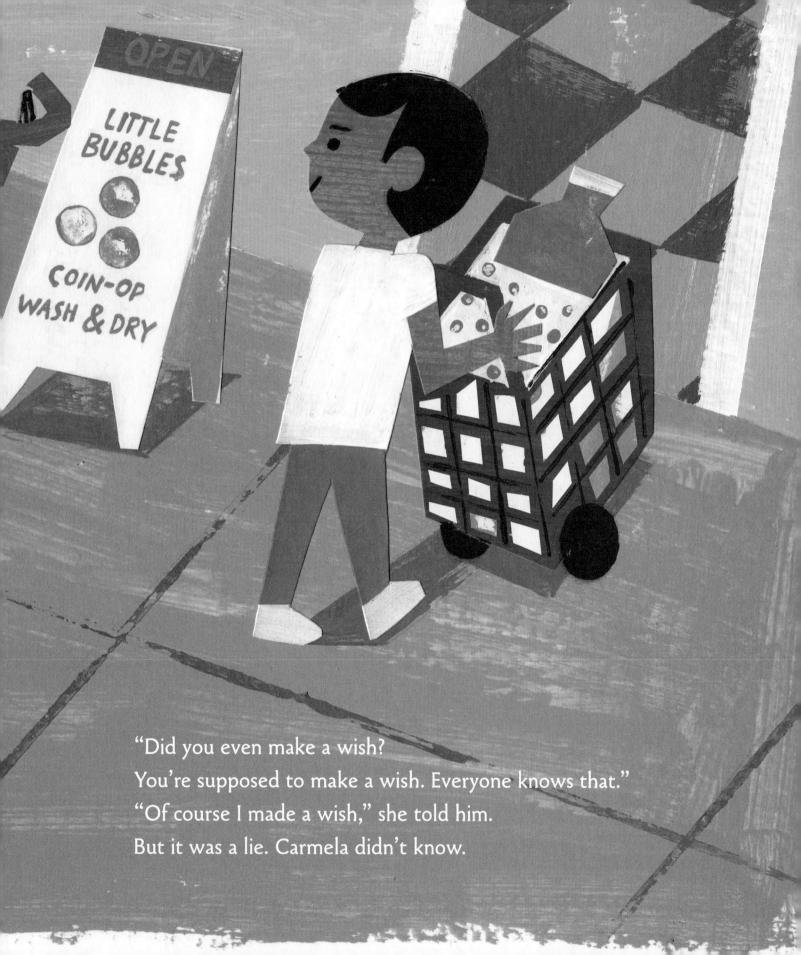

"Did you even make a wish?
You're supposed to make a wish. Everyone knows that."
"Of course I made a wish," she told him.
But it was a lie. Carmela didn't know.

Carmela helped her brother sort colors one-handed,
helped him load the washers one item at a time.
While their clothes spun, her imagination turned,
each new thought ushered in by a jingle of bracelets.

Her brother found the sound annoying
and shot her a dirty look.
Too bad! she told him with her glare.

She jingled her bracelets
as she rode up to Miss Maria's vegetable stand,

imagining a machine built into her bedroom wall,
one that would spit out anything she could think of.
But mostly candies.

She jingled her bracelets
in line at the locksmith shop,

imagining her mom sleeping in one of those fancy hotel beds
she spent all day making for fancy guests.

She jingled her bracelets
at the bodega down the block
from their old apartment building,

imagining her dad getting his papers fixed
so he could finally be home.

She jingled her bracelets
outside the pharmacy,
eyeing the shiny new bikes in the window.
Her brother stopped in his tracks.

"Why do you have to be so annoying?"
She thrummed her bracelets at him and said,
"It's a free country."

The only time she didn't reach for her bracelets
was when her brother ducked into his friend's house.
Carmela slumped down on the curb, silently imagining
all the things she could turn him into.
The slimy pink tail of a rat.
A cockroach scurrying away from the light.
A wheelbarrow full of manure left in the sun.

She stared down at the dandelion in her hand.
It seemed so much more important
now that she knew it was a place to put her wishes.
What if she made the wrong choice?

Carmela tried to hop a curb
on the long trip home,

but her tire caught
and her handlebars twisted
and she went crashing to the concrete.

Don't cry, don't cry, don't cry!
But then she saw her dandelion
crushed beside the drain.

She looked up at her big brother,
warm tears rolling down her cheeks.
He lifted up her scooter. "You okay?"
She shook her head and pointed. "My wish."

He took her by the arm and led her back up the block,
past the Laundromat and the flea market,
past the greenhouses and the smell of manure,
past the overgrown park and across the train tracks.

He didn't stop until they made it to an abandoned
farmhouse near a cliff overlooking the sea.
"Close your eyes," he said.

Carmela closed them.

"Now make your wish," he said.

Carmela listened to the ocean's hum in the distance.

She listened to the squawking birds.

She listened to the wind whistling past her ears.

Then she opened her eyes.
She saw hundreds of tiny white spores lifting
into the air, floating out toward the far-off surf.

The sky was full of wishes.

"Let's go," her brother said.
"Don't you want to know my wish?" she asked.
He shook his head. "If you tell, it won't come true."

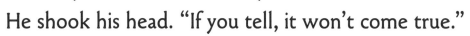

She looked back one last time,
then took off her bracelets and followed her brother home.